From My Heart to Your Heart

Ina Robbins

Illustrated by Anne J. Gavitt

PAULIST PRESS
New York and Mahwah, NJ

Library of Congress Cataloging-in-Publication Data

Robbins, Ina,   1951-
    From my heart to your heart / Ina Robbins ; illustrated by Anne J. Gavitt.
        p.   cm.
    Summary: Lissa and Mama use lines to show the connection they feel between them, even when they are apart.
    ISBN 0-8091-6619-4
    [1. Mother and child—Fiction.]   I. Gavitt, Anne, ill.   II. Title
PZ7.R5326Fr   1994   94-19538
[E]—dc20   CIP
                                                                                        AC

Published by Paulist Press
997 Macarthur Boulevard
Mahwah, New Jersey 07430

Printed and bound in the
United States of America

DEDICATION

To Douglas Frank, my husband, for insisting
I write

"Mama, draw with me," said Lissa as she peered up through the frames of her pink glasses.

"That one looks like a dinosaur head," Mama commented as she peeked over Lissa's shoulder at today's art project.

"It's a mountain, silly." Lissa pulled a stool beside her and patted its seat. "Here, Mama. You can draw the elephants climbing up the mountain."

Mama sat down, but her knees couldn't fit under the table. She straddled the stool as if she was riding a pony.

Lissa smiled. "I know. I'll make the shapes and you can color them in." She liked it when Mama did what she told her to do.

Mama and Lissa drew side by side for some time with only a few words softly spoken between them.

Mama drew a green line from one shape to another. Then she drew another green line connecting two more shapes. Soon she was drawing lines between all the shapes.

Lissa asked, "Mama, why are you drawing lines from picture to picture?"

Mama said, "I'm drawing lines between our pictures—just like the line between me and you."

Lissa thought as she drew, nose to the page. As she changed crayons, she picked up her head and asked, "Mama, how can there be a line between you and me when I leave you to go to school?"

"It stretches," Mama said.

"But, I don't see a line."

"It's invisible," Mama said.

"Where is it?"

"It goes from my heart to your heart." Mama's eyes twinkled.

"But, Mama, I don't feel it."

"It's there." Mama assured her. "If you pay close attention you'll notice it."

Lissa wondered about Mama's moist eyes and then continued coloring. They drew together until the entire page was covered with shapes that looked like ornaments in every color of the crayon box.

In the car the next morning, Lissa asked, "Mama, what will happen to our line after you drop me off at school?"

Mama grinned. "Well, why don't you pay attention and see for yourself?"

"Okay. I will!" Lissa snatched her lunch basket and a kiss, and skipped onto the playground.

That evening, as Mama started dinner, Lissa appeared by her side. "Mama, can I help cook?"

"Sure. How about snipping off the tips of these string beans? I'll rinse the lettuce." Lissa put on her apron and pushed her step stool over to the kitchen counter.

Mama and Lissa worked side by side preparing dinner for some time with only a few words softly spoken between them.

Soon there was a pile of crisp cut string beans on Lissa's cutting board.

Lissa began to line the string beans up, one after another, from her cutting board to Mama's cutting board.

Mama asked, "Why are you making a string bean line from your cutting board to my cutting board?"

Lissa said, "I'm making a line between our boards—just like the line between you and me."

"Oh." Mama tried to hide her smile. "But Liss, how can there be a line between you and me when I leave you to go to work?"

"It's a very long line."

"But I can't see it."

"Maybe you need glasses, Mama." Lissa giggled.

"Well, where is this line any-way?"

"It goes from my heart to your heart." Lissa beamed.

"O-oh, that must be that funny
feeling I have when we're apart!"

"What funny feeling?"

"Well, I feel this little tugging right here," Mama said, holding the palm of her hand to her chest. "Just as if my heart is a fishing pole and I've got a nibble on the line."

"Oh, Mama! It's me! I'm the nibble! I paid attention and I felt the line, just as you said!" Lissa bubbled over as Mama reeled her into a hug and kissed her catch.

Mama released Lissa and they returned to the business of fixing their meal. Mama began tearing the lettuce for a salad. Lissa gathered the row of beans into fistfuls as she put them into the steamer basket.

"Mama? Will that line always be there?

"Even when I grow up?"

As Mama sprinkled a handful of sprouts over the lettuce she looked at Lissa.

"I expect so, Liss. So long as we both keep paying close attention to it. I expect so."

A NOTE TO PARENTS

Lissa's simple story reminds us of the unseen ties we feel between ourselves and our children.

When we play peek-a-boo with our one year old we are teaching that when we go away we will come back. These playful lessons form the foundation of what is known as object constancy, the continuity of relatedness over place and time, which is thought to be an important basis for the ability to form satisfying intimate relationships in adult life. A true gift from the heart.